Completely Crazy Poems

Also compiled by John Foster

A Century of Children's Poems
101 Favourite Poems

Loopy Limericks
Ridiculous Rhymes
Dead Funny
Teasing Tongue-Twisters
Seriously Scary Poems

Completely Crazy Poems

Picked by John Foster

Illustrated by Nathan Reed

Collins

An imprint of HarperCollinsPublishers

First published in Great Britain by Collins 2003
Collins is an imprint of HarperCollins*Publishers* Ltd,
77-85 Fulham Palace Road, Hammersmith, W6 8JB

The HarperCollins website address is:
www.**fire**and**water**.com

1 3 5 7 9 8 6 4 2

This edition copyright © John Foster 2003
Illustrations by Nathan Reed 2003
The acknowledgements on page 95-96
constitute an extension of this copyright page.

0 00 714802 X

Printed and bound in England by
Clays Ltd, St Ives plc

Contents

IF BUDGERIGARS LAID OSTRICH EGGS

IN CUCKOO STREET

COCKROACH CORNFLAKES, TOENAILS FRIED

I'D LIKE TO BE A TEABAG

ONCE UPON A TIME MACHINE

IF BUDGERIGARS
LAID OSTRICH
EGGS

The Battle of the Rattle

Two rattlesnakes were playing pool
The balls were nicely spread
Instead of using wooden cues
They chalked each other's head.

One rattler paused to shed his scales
Then slithered up to win
The other snakes were all agreed
He'd played out of his skin!

Granville Lawson

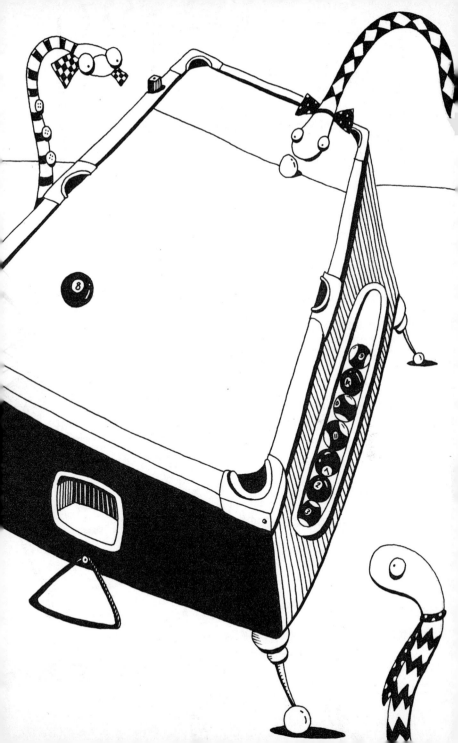

At the Hop

There's a rattlesnake knees-up
In the barn tonight,
Everyone's bopping
To the glow-worms' light.
There's a lizard on guitar
A newt on the drums,
A tortoise on piano
(But he's playing with his thumbs!)
Myrtle the turtle is giving us a twirl,
While Jeremy the python
Is attempting to unfurl.
Nick the iguana
Is sitting on a stool,
Tapping his fingers
And trying to look cool!
Hermione the frog
Is crooning in the corner,
Spurning all advances
From the toad who adores her.

With eyes tight shut and fingers snapping
She's sure got rhythm
When her toes are a-tapping!
Cruising through the dancers
Wearing trendy shades,
Glides Georgie the gecko
On his roller blades.

The whole place is humming
'Til the early morning light,
When the rattlesnakes call it a day
(Or a night!)
They shake their tails loud and clear,
So everyone drinks the last drops of beer,
Then with a slither and a slide,
A creep and a crawl,
They all head homeward
From the rattlesnake ball.

Anne Logan

Love Story

A very old wrinkled iguana
Fell in love with a toothless piranha.
'If we marry,' he said,
'We can live in a shed
And eat sponge cake and mashed-up banana.'

Cynthia Rider

Chess

I play chess with my cheetah.
My cheetah's name is Jim.
He has been known to beat me.
But, mostly, I beat him.

Yesterday I was defeated.
That's because my cheetah cheated.

Kaye Umansky

Elephants

Elephants are bashful,
As bashful as can be.
They always keep their trunks on
When swimming in the sea.

How unlike the polar bears,
Who do not seem to mind
And swim in freezing waters
With a polar bare behind.

Kaye Umanksy

Bears Don't Like Bananas

Monkeys like to play the drums,
badgers wear bandannas.
Tigers like to tickle toes
but bears don't like bananas.

A crocodile can juggle buns
on visits to his Nana's.
Seagulls like to dance and sing
but bears don't like bananas.

Rats and mice can somersault
and do gymnastics with iguanas.
Weasels like to wiggle legs
but bears don't like bananas.

A porcupine likes drinking tea
and cheering at gymkhanas.
A ladybird likes eating pies
but bears don't like bananas.

John Rice

Budgerigars

If budgerigars laid ostrich eggs
They'd have to stretch their little legs
They'd grunt and groan
They'd gasp for air
And end up in intensive care.

Granville Lawson

I Had a Little Pet

I had a little pet
A rather dull brown worm.
To make him look more lovely
I gave him a home-perm.

Colin Thompson

Last Night I Took My Lobster

Last night I took my lobster
For a walk in the midday sun
And we met a diplodocus
Eating a ten tonne raspberry bun.

We met a woolly wombat
Sitting on a beach
We politely asked what time it was
And it offered us a peach.

We met a rhino in a suit
Dancing with a bear
We said the tide was coming in
But they didn't seem to care.

We met a charming Tiger Shark
Reading fairy tales
To a family of porpoises
And some Hump-backed whales.

We met a troop of marmosets
Playing in a band
And watched amazed as bandicoots
Danced tangos in the sand.

Yes, it really was quite wonderful!
It really was such fun!
The night I took my lobster
For a walk in the midday sun!

Tony Langham

Next Door's Cat

Next door's cat has a stripey coat,
it also wears black wellies.
It lost its thermal underwear
so now it borrows Nellie's.

Next door's cat has a bath each night,
it dives into the basin.
We keep a saucer full of milk
for it to wash its face in!

John Rice

Feeling Peckish

My greedy sister
turned into a hen.

She was looking in the biscuit tin
for cookies
when her fingers turned to feathers
and her arms to wings.

Now she lives in the garden
pecking cabbage stalks and things
that hens like to eat.

She claws the lawn for worms
with her scaly feet.

Irene Rawnsley

Don't Marry Your Horse

Whatever you do dear,
Don't marry that horse.
I've heard from a very reliable source
That life in a stable
Is vulgar and coarse.

And, anyway, how
Could you marry a horse
Who'd have you drink water
And eat grass and gorse
With no meat-n-gravy
Or horseradish sauce?

My sweet, I implore you,
Don't marry that horse.
I'm sure there's a law
That the courts can enforce
To stop it and spare you
The pain of divorce.

You can find something better
To wed than a horse.
I'll tap it out, letter
By letter, in Morse:
Don't marry, don't marry,
Don't marry that horse.

Nick Toezek

Wacky Wild Animals

My dad's wacky about animals.
He breeds them
and he cross breeds them.

He crossed a gorilla with a poodle.
Now we've got a Goroodle.
Seven feet tall and very fierce
But it wears pink ribbons in its shaved fur.

Then he crossed a snake with a dog.
We've got a Snog.
Very friendly, but no-one wants to kiss it.

After that he tried a cat and a parrot.
That was boring.
We got a Carrot.

Dad found the cross between the Guinea Pig
  and the hare very useful.
It lives on his bald head.
The Guinea Wig.

He crossed a squirrel and a worm.
Now he's got a long pink hairy squirm from
   the Wirral.

He crossed some ants with a pig.
Now he's got some pants that grunt.

Then he tried crossing a mynah bird with a herd
   of bullocks...
and got a bird that talks a load of baloney.

Mum made dad stop though.
She didn't like it when he tried crossing
the elephant and the duck.
And believe me when it flies over your head
...you have to.

Paul Cookson and David Harmer

The Fumbletwit

A formal bird, the Fumbletwit,
He tried with all his might
To be just like his neighbours
But he never got things right.

So formal was the Fumbletwit
That much of his time was spent
Bowing low to say, 'How d' you do?'
So his beak got rather bent.

And since his beak was very sore
He could not build a nest;
He laid his eggs upon the floor
Or tucked them up his vest.

And when at last his babies hatched
And squawked their hungry squawk,
Because his beak was far from straight,
He fed them with a fork.

'He's showing off!' cried Crow and Rook
'That bird is such a snob!
That's not the way to shove a worm
Into your baby's gob!'

Oh pity the poor Fumbletwit!
He wanted to be normal,
Yet his neighbours mocked him night and day
For being far too formal.

But he finally moved to the Falklands
Where there was no such fuss,
For the penguins (who dressed for dinner) said,
'Ah! He is one of us!'

Ian Whybrow

Par For the Course

When Auntie Fay began to neigh
And spend the day just eating hay,
My uncle said, 'It's par for the course.
Your Auntie has become a horse.
I'll have to put her in the stable,
In the stall next to your Auntie Mabel!'

John Foster

IN CUCKOO STREET

The Curlapop
(after Milligan)

'What *is* a Curlapop, Dad?'
'It's a kind of a snake
Which lives in a box
And wears frilly socks
When it goes for a swim in the lake.'

'What does a Curlapop do, Dad?'
'It plays football with fleas.
It eats jellied eels
While turning cartwheels
And sings songs as it swings through the trees.'

'Have you seen a Curlapop, Dad?'
'On a day-trip to France,
In the town of Calais,
In a street café,
I once saw a Curlapop dance.'

'Are you sure there's a Curlapop, Dad?'

'Without any doubt, my son.

I swear by the moon

That goes green in June.

I'll take bets at a thousand to one.'

John Foster

In Cuckoo Street

Down one way clocks in Cuckoo Street,
Where racing cakes drive chocolate cars,
Old string mice in sugar vests
Are shooting jam at strawberry stars.

Beneath baked skies and blue potatoes,
April ducks, like rubber fools,
Are drinking fish through jelly straws,
Swimming in their wine red pools.

But feather pigs wave guinea dusters,
Moon away the sweeping beams,
While bedtime gnomes tell garden stories
In sweet baths that bubble dreams.

Celia Warren

Skangaloo

'In Skangaloo,' our teacher said,
'they all wear chickens on their heads
to keep them warm when cold winds blow
and Skangaloo is pink with snow.
In Skangaloo, where mammoths roam,
people catch a mammoth home.
A bus is cosier, it's true,
but seldom seen in Skangaloo.
In Skangaloo the Dodo bird
is ever seen and always heard
and honks right through the star bright night
beneath the twin moons' silver light.'
'Twin moons?' a doubting schoolgirl cried.
Our teacher frowned. 'I haven't lied.
I know all this because I too,
lived long ago in Skangaloo.'
He placed his chicken on his head.
'It's home time now,' our teacher said.
'So wrap up warm and off you go.

It looks as if it's going to snow.
Oh Skangaloo,' he murmured, 'why
do I think of you and sigh.
Where now is the way back to
the purple plains of Skangaloo?'

Marian Swinger

Who Am I?

My face fell off my head
and landed on the floor,
wriggled about a while
then galloped out the door.

It scared a cat in the yard.
It ate some bread and jam.
It fell into a puddle –
now I don't know who I am.

Michael Rosen

Flo's Toe

Auntie Flo
Has a Magic Toe
Which SHINES OUT in the gloom;
If she wakes with fright
In the middle of the night
Her Toe LIGHTS UP THE ROOM!

Trevor Harvey

Nathaniel

Nathaniel woke up yawning,
'I'm half asleep,' he said,
So his left half went down to breakfast
And his right half stayed in bed.

Richard Edwards

My Sister Turned Into Barbie

My sister turned into Barbie

It happened in the night

By breakfast she had gone all stiff

And her skirt was much too tight

She started wearing pink a lot
And silly purple pumps
Where once a vest covered her chest
She now had plastic lumps

Her hair became a flaxen rope
Which hung down to her knees
Her knickers they were welded on
So she couldn't go for pees

She started hanging out with Ken
Blew bubbles from her head
We had to straighten out her limbs
To get her into bed

Life was becoming a pink plastic nightmare so...

We took her to the toy shop
When she turned weird under water
My mum said: 'Take this flipping thing
And give me back my daughter!'

Lindsay MacRae

Aunty Aggie

Cleaning round the house one day,
Aunty Aggie went astray;
Sucked up by the vacuum cleaner,
Since which time, no one has seen her.
Where she is, there's no knowing,
But when the thing was overflowing,
It seems to me without a doubt,
They simply threw the old bag out.

Mike Jubb

The Day the Fridge Turned on Uncle Stan

For twenty years my uncle Stan
kept his fridge both spic and span,
so when the fridge said it was freezing
Stan thought at first that it was teasing.
'All I do is stand and shiver,'
said the fridge, its voice a-quiver,
'stuffed with all your food and beer';
it dropped a sad and frozen tear.
'That's all you're for,' my uncle said,
as laughter filled his vacant head.
'A fridge has got no heart or soul,
all it does is keep things cold.'
As he laughed, the fridge rebelled,
with tentacles of ice it held
my uncle tight, his cheeky grin
freezing as they dragged him in.

Michael Dugan

The Toilet Seat Has Teeth!

The bathroom has gone crazy
far beyond belief.
The sink is full of spiders
and the toilet seat has teeth!

The plughole in the bath
has a whirlpool underneath
that pulls you down feet first
and the toilet seat has teeth!

The toothpaste tube is purple
and makes your teeth fall out.
The toilet roll is nettles
and makes you scream and shout!

The towels have got bristles,
the bubble bath is glue,
the soap has turned to jelly
and it makes your skin bright blue.

The hot tap gushes forth
with a sludge that is bright pink.
The cold tap dribbles lumps
of green that block the sink.

The mirror's pulling faces
at everyone it can.
The shower's dripping marmalade
and blackcurrant jam.

The rubber ducks are breeding
and building their own nest
with shaving foam and tissues
in Grandad's stringy vest.

Shampoo is liquid dynamite,
there's petrol in the hairspray,
both will cure dandruff
when they blow your head away!

The bathroom has gone crazy
far beyond belief.
The sink is full of spiders
and the toilet seat has teeth!

Paul Cookson

Mr Dishcloth Man's Gang – a Bunch of Dirty Villains

Mr Dustpan had several brushes with the law

Mr Dirty Water Man saw his career go down the drain

Mr Vacuum Cleaner Man found himself on the carpet

Mr Toilet Cleaner went right round the bend

Yes

Mr Dishcloth Man's gang were all washed up.

John Coldwell

Coathanger

I gave my love a coathanger,

She flung it back at me.

It acted like a boomerang

and hit her on the knee.

Colin West

A Lazy Young Phantom
Called Pete

A lazy young phantom called Pete
Went for weeks without changing his sheet.
When Pete went 'Boo!'
Everybody cried 'Poo!'
And ran for fresh air in the street.

Kaye Umansky

Clanky Franky

In Clanky Franky's garden
flowers clatter in the breeze
and rusty leaves come rattling down
from aluminium trees.
But it's a quiet garden,
he oils it every day
and greases the hinged branches so they don't creak when they sway.
He dibbles with a high-speed drill in beds of polished metal
to plant bright stalks of stainless steel
then screws on every petal.
He solders on brassberries,
he tightens up each nut,
his grass is green – but copper
so it never   needs a cut.
No dirt, no weeds,   no nibbling bugs –
it's so easy   to maintain;
but like any   other gardener
Franky loves   to complain
of the rubber cats   and plastic gnats
and most of all   ...the rain

Dave Calder

John Spoon

John Spoon dressed up in camouflage,
In brown and blotchy green,
And lay down in a grassy field
To keep from being seen.

But camouflage is dangerous,
And camouflage is how
Poor Johnny Spoon one afternoon
Got eaten by a cow.

Richard Edwards

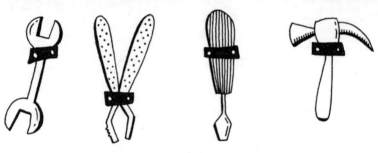

Jeremy Kettle

Jeremy Kettle is made out of metal,
His jacket is bright shiny steel.
With his shoes full of screws
He can hardly move:
So he has to drink oil with each meal.

He lives off stale crusts
Made from girders and rust;
Wears brass washers instead of a ring:
But Jeremy Kettle can sit on a nettle
Without ever feeling a thing!

David Greygoose

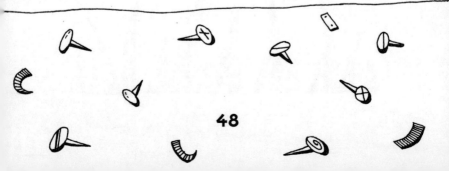

William Y-Front

William Y-Front could never go out
he could never play ball in the park,
for he'd been born in the shape of orange underpants
which glowed every night in the dark.

People would stop to catch just a glimpse,
they would wait at his house every day,
for a first look at William Y-Front
and that dazzling orange display.

Until poor William could take it no more
and so ran away right out to sea,
where he now has a job as a lighthouse
somewhere off the coast of Torquay.

Andrew Collett

COCKROACH CORNFLAKES, TOENAILS FRIED

What Monsters Eat For Breakfast

Cockroach cornflakes covered in mould
Fat from the grill pan, five weeks old
Poltergeist dribble on pulverised toast
Four fried toes of a hairy ghost

Lumps of grobbit with Dracula jam
All mixed up in a rusty pram
Six slug sausages, nice and pink
Wash it all down with a cold sick drink

Roger Stevens and Michael Leigh

Lunchtime Treat

My neighbour, Mister Hare,
clips his toenails with great care,
and fries in oil or dripping
what he saves from every clipping.
Toenails fried, he says, while munching
are his favourite dish for lunching.

Michael Dugan

The Wild Yorkshire Pudding

On moors we are hunting
The wild Yorkshire pudding;
The small ones are nippy,
The fat ones are grunting.

They snuggle together
And hide in the heather;
The young ones are tasty,
The old ones like leather.

We jump on and snatch 'em;
They shriek as we catch 'em;
On cords which take twenty
We string and attach 'em.

They dry them in Batley;
They can them in Ilkley.
You will find they are served
Where menus are stately.

Our terriers are scenting
The rock-crevice-skulking
Tremendous with gravy
And wild Yorkshire pudding.

Alan Dixon

Anti-gravity Gravy

Anti-gravity gravy
is wonderful. It's new.
And yes, of course, it's just the sauce
to liven up a stew.

Anti-gravity gravy
will fill you with delight,
for, if you take it with your lunch
you'll end up feeling light.

Anti-gravity gravy
will keep your spirits up.
But when you're trying to stir it,
it won't stay in the cup.

It's fabulous, it's flavoursome,
it's groovy and it's great.
The only problem is it simply
won't stay on the plate.

It spirals slowly upwards
to float above the table,
so put some on your mashed potatoes
if you think you're able.

It rises and it hovers
and drifts about with ease.
You'll puzzle over how to pour it
neatly on your peas.

Anti-gravity gravy
may serve up a surprise
by gushing from the gravy-boat
and squirting in your eyes.

But, of its quirky qualities,
the thing you'll find the worst,
is, if you want to try it,
you'll have to catch it first.

Tony Mitton

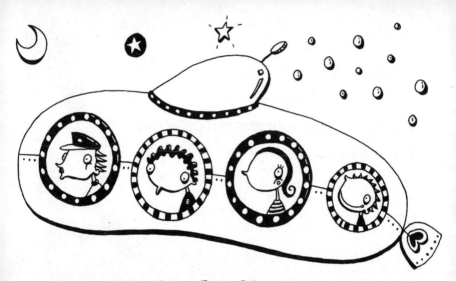

One Night At Noon

On a dark dreary night
At twelve o'clock noon,
A knife and a fork
Turned into a spoon.

A satellite sank
And a submarine flew
And twenty-six camels
Ate daffodil stew.

Clive Webster

58

Jelly Hair

As I was going from here to there
I saw a man with Jelly Hair.
It wibbled as he walked along,
And wobbled like a springy-sprong.
I wondered, 'Does it ever grow,
Or does it melt away like snow?'
– And if that Jelly Hair *did* melt
How terrible it must have felt
All dripping down his face and nose
And forming puddles round his toes.
And people looking at the ground
Would think a monster was around,
For large wet footprints would be seen
In slimy, slippy, jelly green.
– I think, if asked, I would prefer
To have my own, not Jelly Hair.

Margot Bosonnet

Three Cannibals

Said the cannibal, 'I'm in the mood
To have some of our friends round for food.'
Said his wife, 'Yes, my dear,
That's a brilliant idea.
Would you like them boiled, roasted or stewed?'

'Can I serve you a nice cut of beef?'
Said the waiter to the cannibal chief.
'No, I want something human,
Like a large slice of you, man,
To follow the aperitif.'

The cannibal returned yesterday
With an arm and a leg gone astray.
He explained this strange lack
By declaring, 'I'm back
From a self-catering holiday.'

Eric Finney

Rumbletum Rapples

Rumbletum Rapples
loved nothing but apples
which he ate day in and day out.
One day his boots
turned into roots
and his ears began to sprout.
Three branches arose
from his arms and his nose
and leaves began to appear.
Now Rumbletum Rapples
is covered in apples
though they taste a trifle queer.

Michael Dugan

The Toffee Mine

Invest in toffee mines? I hear
That's not all a good idea.
It's there in tons, oh right enough,
But how to shift the beastly stuff.
In any kind of warmish weather
One's pick and shovel stick together.

No sooner do the miners start
Than tools must all be licked apart.
Just think of all the time it takes
And all the awful tummy aches.
And not just that... it clogs the hair,
Eyebrows, fingers, everywhere.
It clogs your socks, your boots, your laces.
It gets in most unlikely places.
Imagine if you can, the smell
Of mint, vanilla, caramel.
And on a sticky summer's day
The fumes would make you swoon away.

How sad the toffee miner's lot,
To have such wealth yet have it not.
He guards his hoard but lives in doubt
That he will ever get it out.

Michael Comyns

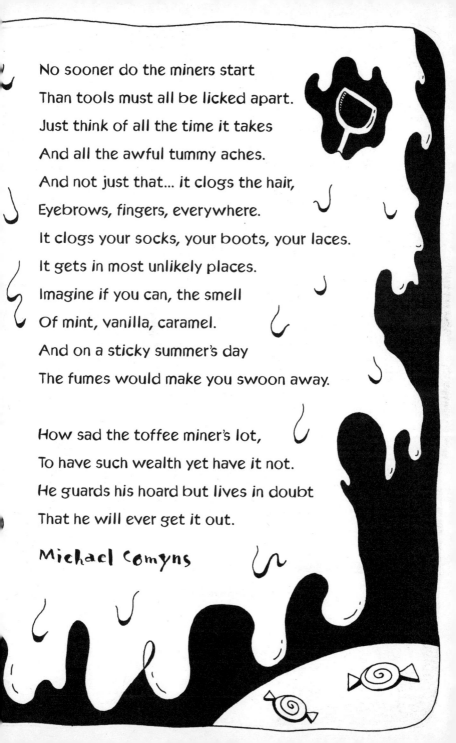

Manners

Don't eat custard with your fingers
When invited out to tea.
It isn't right, it's not polite.
Eat your fingers separately!

Kaye Umansky

I'D LIKE TO
BE A TEABAG

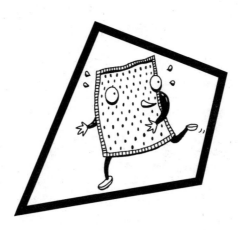

I'd Like To Be a Teabag

I'd like to be a teabag,
And stay at home all day –
And talk to other teabags
In a teabag sort of way...

I'd love to be a teabag,
And lie in a little box –
And never have to wash my face
Or change my dirty socks...

I'd like to be a teabag,
An Earl Grey one perhaps,
And doze all day and lie around
With Earl Grey kind of chaps.

I wouldn't have to do a thing,
No homework, jobs or chores –
Comfy in my caddy
Of teabags and their snores.

I wouldn't have to do exams,

I needn't tidy rooms,

Or sweep the floor or feed the cat

Or wash up all the spoons.

I wouldn't have to do a thing,

A life of bliss – you see...

Except that once in all my life

I'd make a cup of tea!

Peter Dixon

My Auntie Dot

My Auntie Dot's a coffee pot.
She sits on the kitchen shelf,
Waiting for someone to take her down,
Quietly polishing herself.

'To be a coffee pot's my lot,'
She says. 'It's rather boring.
There's nothing to do, while I sit here,
I can't even practise my pouring.'

'A coffee pot is not what
I'd be if I could choose.
My sister's son has far more fun,
'Cause he's a pair of shoes!'

John Foster

A Boy Named Bubbles

The day I turned into a washing up liquid bottle
Mum said,
'Let's have a look at you.'
She took me into the kitchen,
Turned me upside down
And squeezed.
'Empty. I might have known.
You want to buck your ideas up lad.
And don't think you're having a day off school.'

In the playground, everybody called me 'Bubbles'.
and tried to pull my cap off.
It was our class's turn to go swimming.
I got top marks for floating.
In Drama, I played the part of a truncheon.
That hurt.
In Science, Rachel stuck cardboard fins on me
and chucked me across the room —
An experiment in aerodynamics.
That hurt too.
I couldn't do Maths,
I had a headache.

John Coldwell

There Was a Young Man of Devizes

There was a young man of Devizes,
Whose ears were of different sizes;
One was quite small,
And of no use at all,
But the other was huge and won prizes.

Anon

The Young Man Who Couldn't See Why

There was a young man who asked 'Why
Can't I look in my ear with my eye?
If I put my mind to it
I'm sure I could do it.
You never can tell till you try!'

Anon

Eileen Idle

Eileen Idle's eyebrows,
The hairiest of features,
Make the perfect hiding place
For shy little creatures.

Deep in Eileen's eyebrows,
Fieldmice meet for talks,
And wrens enjoy a game of cards
Safe from sparrowhawks.

Richard Edwards

Knotty Girl

A young yoga fanatic called Christa
Who was showing off a trick to her sister
Became stuck for a year
With her toe in her ear
Till they managed, at last, to untwist her.

Colin Macfarlane

Norman Norton's Nostrils

Oh, Norman Norton's Nostrils
Are powerful and strong;
Hold on to your belongings
If he should come along.

And do not ever let him
Inhale with all his might,
Or else your pens and pencils
Will disappear from sight.

Right up his nose they'll vanish
Your future will be black.
Unless he gets the sneezes
You'll never get them back.

Colin West

The Young Girl of Asturias

There was a young girl of Asturias,
Whose temper was frantic and furious.
She used to throw eggs
At her grandmother's legs –
A habit unpleasant, but curious.

Anon

I Wish I Were a Dozen Eggs

I wish I were a dozen eggs
Sitting in a tree
And when you passed along below
I'd splatter you with me.

Anon

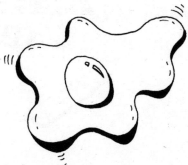

ONCE uPON A TIME MACHINE

Once Upon a Time Machine

Once upon a time machine

I woke up screaming, in a dream:

The strawberry jam had turned bright green,

The king and queen were wearing jeans,

And all the flowers ate ice cream;

Once upon a time machine.

Once upon a time machine
I wondered what it was I'd seen:
A pillow filled with pink baked beans,
A snowman made of margarine,
And a robot in a football team;
Once upon a time machine.

Once upon a time machine
I asked myself what did it mean:
On a walking, talking TV screen,
A saucepan swimming in a stream,
A sun-dial stone which struck thirteen,
And cold mince pies at Hallowe'en;
Once upon a time machine.

David Greygoose

Auntie Diluvian and Uncle Orang

Auntie Diluvian and
Uncle Orang
are strange,
fascinating and sweet.
Auntie is shrivelled
and mumbles all day
whilst Uncle
likes picking his feet.

Auntie's wild stories
enthral me, and yet
my family believes
not a word.
But I know
she once
punched a dinosaur,
and also met Richard III.

Uncle is quieter
with very long arms,
most skilled in
the naming of trees.
And when we're asleep
he sits on the fridge
peacefully
sucking his fleas.

Auntie draws pictures
of things that she's seen,
of crossbows,
of floods and stampedes.
She hand-reared a dodo
and also a clown
by feeding them
lollipop seeds.

Uncle is ready
to help with odd jobs,
his favourite is
sweeping up leaves.
And if he wore clothes,
from the way that he walks
he'd always be
trailing his sleeves.

Even in sunlight
Auntie smells damp
with steam coming off
her old coat.
She blames that on Noah
for sailing too soon,
that, and a
very full boat.

Uncle is stringy,
thoughtful, serene,
his fur
a continuing flame.
He's also forgetful,
and loses things like
the disappeared half
of his name.

Auntie Diluvian
and Uncle Orang
enjoy playing
musical chairs.
But when it rains hard
Auntie goes quiet
whilst Uncle hides
under the stairs.

Stewart Henderson

Fast Fruit and Veg

Uncle Sid drives a very fast marrow

My dad rides a smart purple plum.

He went away for a week

And came back on a leek

With an open-top courgette for Mum!

Trevor Millum

Dorothy Porridge

Dorothy Porridge is wearing a lettuce
And nobody quite knows why,
She's racing around like the spin of a coin
And waving her fist at the sky.
The last time I saw her she lifted a leaf
And gave me a wink of her eye,
Dorothy Porridge is wearing a lettuce
And nobody quite knows why.

Richard Edwards

The Elusive Beetroot

They seek him here, they seek him there,

They seek that beetroot everywhere.

He's rooted off and disappeared,

The reddest beetroot of the year,

A trail of crimson all around,

That beetroot's covered lots of ground.

Will they find him, will they not?

Will that beetroot cheat the pot?

Or will he, just like all the others,

Be boiled and sugared for beetroot lovers,

And disappear down some fat tum?

So run old beetroot, run, run, run!

Elusive as the Pimpernel,

Run red beetroot, run like...!

Clive Webster

Space Traveller

I journeyed into outer space.
I was lucky to have survived.
Travelling faster than the speed of light
I got back before I'd arrived!

Nigel Gray

The Chocolate Soldier

A chocolate soldier crossed the road
When the lights were red
A double decker bus came by
And now he's chocolate spread.

Granville Lawson

Clothes on the Motorway

Pants on the motorway, chasing trucks and cars
Motorists distracted by knickers and bras
Gloves thumbing lifts, shirts hitching rides
Together with trousers with patched backsides
Bikinis relaxing, sunbathing on the grass
Spotted hankies waving at the lorries that pass
Dozens of dresses, frocks and socks
Piling up to look like police road blocks
Three piece suits hanging up on traffic signs
Pairs of tights pretending to be double yellow lines
Jumpers thumping bumpers and denting chrome

But the sensible shoes are walking home.

John Coldwell

The Jigglybusters

On the moon, in holes and craters,
looking like immense potatoes,
huddled up in knobbly clusters,
live the mournful Jigglybusters.
Each has six eyes on waving stalks
which glow bright yellow as they talk,
each has twenty big flat feet
and every day they sit and eat
a heap of moondust mixed with rocks.
They wear tall hats and stripey socks
and like to bounce across the moon
light and airy as balloons.
They watch the Earth up in the sky
and as they watch they wail and sigh
and say, 'How lovely if we too
lived on a world of green and blue
instead of eating dust and rocks
and knitting miles of stripey socks
and sleeping in the cold, dark craters
and looking like immense potatoes.'

Marian Swinger

Windscreen Wipers

My windscreen wipers don't want to wipe.
They're old and tired and need a rest.
They've swished and swashed for years and years
they think they've done their best.

So I took them off and brought them home
and gave them each a chair.
They sit and watch old movies,
or simply sit and stare.

They do: 'The Snake Who Cleaned Windows'.
the 'Windscreen Vipers' joke
They talk of scrapes and dangers
like the time the windscreen broke.

They read the papers, have a stretch
and after they have fed
they have a wash, clean their teeth
and settle down in bed.

My windscreen still gets dirty and wet,
it looks smarter than it's been.
Two new wipers, strong and fast
wipe the windscreen clean.

Michael Rosen

Aliens Stole My Underpants

To understand the ways
of alien beings is hard,
and I've never worked it out
why they landed in my backyard.

And I've always wondered why
on their journey from the stars,
these aliens stole my underpants
and took them back to Mars.

They came on a Monday night
when the weekend wash had been done,
pegged out on the line
to be dried by the morning sun.

Mrs Driver from next door
was a witness at the scene
when aliens snatched my underpants –
I'm glad that they were clean!

It seems they were quite choosy
as nothing else was taken.
Do aliens wear underpants
or were they just mistaken?

I think I have a theory
as to what they wanted them for,
they needed to block off a draught
blowing in through the spacecraft door.

Or maybe some Mars museum
wanted items brought back from space.
Just think, my pair of Y-fronts
displayed in their own glass case.

And on the label beneath
would be written where they got 'em
and how such funny underwear
once covered an Earthling's bottom!

Brian Moses

A Ghoulish Proposal

Two ghouls were dancing cheek to cheek
And each admired the other;
The ghoulie boy said, 'Ghoulie girl,
You look just like my mother –
Your bloodshot gaze, your filthy ways,
your grimy, hairy knees –
My ghoulie girl, my ugly one,
Oh will you marry me?'

The ghoulie girl was overcome
At what her partner said;
She blushed a bashful purple
And she punched him in the head.
'You smell of cheese, you're full of fleas,
You're really on the nose...
Oh ghoulie boy, my stinky one,
Let's do as you propose!'

The wedding was at twelve o'clock
The night of Hallowe'en;
The dark was filled with mournful howls
And agonizing screams.
The ghastly two have vowed anew
To fight both loud and often,
And they have put downpayment on
A mouldy double coffin.

Sally Farrell Odgers

Aniseed Annie and Liquorice Lou

Aniseed Annie and Liquorice Lou
Rode into town on a kangaroo.
The kangaroo parked on a double yellow line
And the Traffic Warden gave them a fine.

John Foster

Acknowledgements

We are grateful to the following authors for permission to include the following poems, all of which are published for the first time in this collection:

Dave Calder: 'Clanky Franky' copyright © Dave Calder 2003. John Coldwell: 'A Boy Named Bubbles', 'Mr Dishcloth Man's Gang – A Bunch of Dirty Villains' and 'Clothes on the Motorway' all copyright © John Coldwell 2003. Paul Cookson and David Harmer: 'Wacky Wild Animals' copyright © Paul Cookson and David Harmer 2003. Eric Finney: 'Three Cannibals' copyright © Eric Finney 2003. John Foster: 'Par For the Course', 'The Curlapop', 'My Auntie Dot' and 'Aniseed Annie and Liquorice Lou' all copyright © John Foster 2003. Nigel Gray: 'Space Traveller' copyright © Nigel Gray 2003. David Greygoose: 'Jeremy Kettle' and 'Once Upon a Time Machine' copyright © David Greygoose 2003. Tony Langham: 'Last Night I Took My Lobster' copyright © Tony Langham 2003. Granville Lawson: 'Budgerigars', 'The Battle of the Rattle' and 'The Chocolate Soldier' all copyright © Granville Lawson 2003. Anne Logan: 'At the Hop' copyright © Anne Logan 2003. Colin Macfarlane: 'Knotty Girl' copyright © Colin Macfarlane 2003. Trevor Millum: 'Fast Fruit and Veg' copyright © Trevor Millum 2003. Cynthia Rider: 'Love Story' copyright © Cynthia Rider 2003. Roger Stevens and Michael Leigh: 'What Monsters Eat For Breakfast' copyright © Roger Stevens and Michael Leigh 2003. Marian Swinger: 'Skangaloo' and 'The Jigglybusters' copyright © Marian Swinger 2003. Celia Warren: 'In Cuckoo Street' copyright © Celia Warren 2003. Clive Webster: 'One Night At Noon' and 'The Elusive Beetroot' both copyright © Clive Webster 2003. Ian Whybrow: 'The Fumbletwit' copyright © Ian Whybrow 2003.

We also acknowledge permission to include previously published poems:

Margot Bosonnet: 'Jelly Hair' copyright © Margot Bosonnet from *Skyscraper Ted and Other Zany Verse* (Wolfhound Press, Dublin 1994). Andrew Collett: 'William Y-Front' copyright © 1999 Andrew Collett, from *Bottling Burps For Grandma* (The King's England Press), included by permission of the author. Paul Cookson: 'The Toilet Seat Has Teeth!' copyright © 1992 Paul Cookson, first published in *The Toilet Seat Has Teeth (A Twist in the Tale)*, included by permission of the author. Peter Dixon: 'I'd Like To Be a Teabag' copyright © 1998 Peter Dixon from *The Hippo Book of Silly Poems* (Scholastic), included by permission of the author. Michael Dugan: 'The Day the Fridge Turned On Uncle Stan', 'Lunchtime Treat' and 'Rumbletum Rapples' all copyright ©